The
Emperor's
New Clothes

Retold by Susanna Davidson

Illustrated by Mike Gordon

Reading Consultant: Alison Kelly
Roehampton University

Contents

Chapter 1

Nothing to wear

Once upon a time there was an emperor who *loved* clothes. He really didn't care about anything else.

3

He ignored his soldiers...

avoided his advisors...

hated plays...

...and only liked riding in the park so he could show off his amazing outfits.

You look amazing, Your Excellence.

But the emperor had a problem. The royal procession was in two weeks' time, and he had nothing to wear.

"You must have something, Your Excellence," said Boris, his servant. "You already have seven thousand, three hundred and twenty-two outfits."

"But I've worn them all before," moaned the emperor.

"I want to look so amazing, so fantastic, so *splendiferous*, that people will talk about me for years to come."

"I see," said Boris, looking rather glum. It was Boris who had to take care of all the emperor's clothes.

9

"Are you sure this one won't do?" Boris asked hopefully, picking a velvet and gold suit from the pile.

"Boris," said the emperor, in a stern voice.

"Er, yes, sire?" said Boris.

"Who is the emperor here?"

"You are, Your Excellence,"
replied Boris.

"Right. And if I say I want
new clothes, then I mean it!"

"Go and find me the finest
clothes-makers in town,"
ordered the emperor. "At once!"

"I'm off to have a snooze," the emperor added. "It's been a very tiring morning."

As you wish, Your Excellence.

Chapter 2

Slimus and Slick

FLOUR

URGENT!
Emperor needs
tasteful
and elegant
new outfit!
Clothes-makers
apply here.

Boris spent all day looking for an incredible outfit. He wasn't having much luck, until...

...two strangers rushed up to him. "We're the finest clothes-makers in the world," they said. "Take us to the emperor at once."

When they arrived at the palace, the strangers pushed past the palace footmen and burst into the emperor's room.

"Who are you?" shouted the emperor, angrily. He was busy choosing his afternoon coat and hated being interrupted.

15

"We are Slimus..."

"and Slick..."

"...at your service," they said, and bowed.

The emperor just stared
at them.

"Haven't you heard of us?"
said Slimus, looking shocked.

We're world-
famous!

"Um, well... no," admitted
the emperor. He hated not
knowing things.

17

"We make magical clothes!" said Slimus.

"Magical?" said the emperor, sounding interested.

"Yes," said Slick, with a sly smile. "Our clothes can only be seen by clever people."

"They will be absolutely invisible to anyone stupid," Slimus explained.

"Anyone who can't do their job properly won't be able to see them either," Slick added.

Boris gulped. "What if I can't see the clothes?" he thought.

19

The emperor was very excited. "Make me a magic suit this minute," he cried.

"It won't be cheap," said Slimus and Slick. "We only use the very best material."

"Take this," said the emperor, handing them a sack of money. "You can work in the palace – take anything you want. Only get to work. I want that suit!"

Chapter 3
The two cheats

As soon as they were alone, Slimus and Slick laughed until their bellies ached and their faces turned purple.

21

"The fool believed us!" cried Slimus. "We're going to have lots and lots of *lovely* money."

They set up their looms in the palace and ordered in the finest silks and the most expensive gold thread.

But they didn't use any of it. Instead they sold it all for lots more money.

"Is there anything else you need?" asked the emperor.

"Yes," Slick replied. "Five fudge cakes, ten tubs of vanilla ice cream and a constant supply of chocolate. That would really help our work."

This is the life.

"But you mustn't see a thing until it's finished," Slick told the emperor. "We want it to be a fantastic surprise."

Every day the emperor crept past their door, listening to the loom going back and forth. He was desperate to know how the suit was coming along.

"I know," he thought. "I'll send Boris along to find out."

But when Boris went in, he could see nothing but empty looms.

"What do you think of our wonderful work?" asked Slick.

"Such a charming pattern, isn't it?" said Slimus.

"Oh crumbs," thought Boris.
"I can't see a thing. I must be
stupid."

"Well," demanded Slimus.
"Have you got nothing to say?"

Boris gulped. "It's, er, fantastic," he lied. "Absolutely, um, great. I'll tell the emperor I'm very pleased with it."

I wish I could see it!

He hurried off to tell the emperor how fabulous his new clothes were. Slimus and Slick smiled to themselves, and went back to eating cake.

Chapter 4

The emperor's visit

Word quickly spread through
the kingdom that the emperor
had ordered some amazing
and mysterious new clothes.

And the emperor couldn't wait a moment longer to see them. He called for Boris and the palace footmen, and went to see Slimus and Slick at work.

"Oh Your Excellence," said Slimus, bowing low. "We're so pleased to see you!"

The emperor looked at the loom, then looked again. "This is terrible," he thought. "I can't see anything. I'm not worthy of being emperor!"

But aloud he said, "It's magnificent."

"Really very tasteful," added Boris.

The palace footmen were worried. Each thought the other could see the magic material. "Splendid," they said in unison.

31

Slimus and Slick pretended to take the material down from the loom. They made cuts in the air with huge scissors and sewed using needles without any thread.

Everyone clapped loudly. The emperor even gave Slimus and Slick a gold medal each for their excellent sewing.

On the morning of the royal procession, the emperor went to put on his new clothes. He was filled with nervous excitement.

Here's your coat.

And your pantaloons!

"Would Your Majesty care to undress?" said Slimus. "Then we'll put on your clothes in front of the mirror."

"I'll bring over the cloak," said Slick. "Boris, pick up the train, will you?"

"This is your shirt, Your Majesty," said Slimus. "See, it's as light as a spider's web."

Slick smiled. "Oh it fits *so* well," he said.

Then the palace footmen bent down, just as if they were picking up a train. The emperor admired himself in the mirror one last time.

"Well, I'm ready," he said. "Don't I look splendid, Boris?"

"Yes, Your Excellence," said Boris, looking straight up at the ceiling.

"Then open the palace doors," said the emperor. "Let the royal procession begin."

People won't believe their eyes!

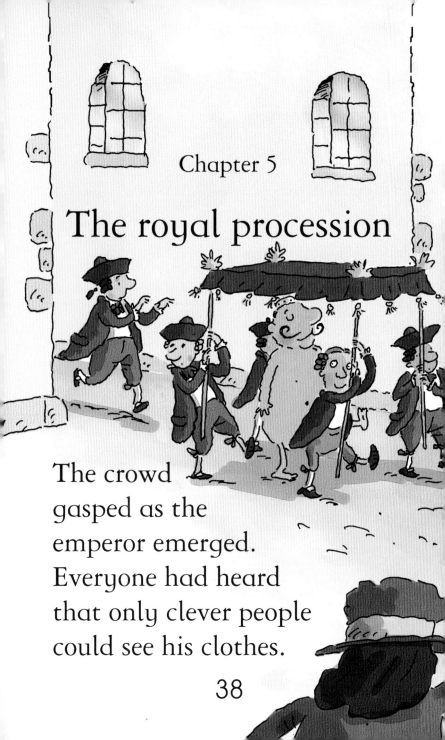

Chapter 5

The royal procession

The crowd
gasped as the
emperor emerged.
Everyone had heard
that only clever people
could see his clothes.

"What a wonderful outfit," they cried.

"Such a magnificent pattern," said a woman.

The emperor smiled to himself. "These are my most successful clothes ever," he thought, and added a spring to his step.

"Let me see him," cried a small child, who was stuck at the back of the crowd.

The child was lifted up on his father's shoulders, so he could see the emperor in all his glory.

"Ooh!" said the child. "The emperor's got nothing on!"

Everyone around the child fell silent and looked at the emperor again.

"He's right you know," said his father. "The emperor is *naked*!"

Then, faster than a spreading fire, a whisper whizzed through the crowd.

The emperor's got no clothes on!

Soon the whole crowd was chanting. "The emperor's got no clothes on!"

The emperor's got no clothes on!

The emperor heard their words and shivered. Suddenly, he felt very cold.

He looked down. To his horror, the emperor saw that they were right.

Then he blushed bright red – all over.

"I must carry on," he thought. "This is the royal procession – and *I* am the emperor."

The emperor held his head high and walked more proudly than ever.

Meanwhile, Slimus and Slick were packing their bags full of money, getting ready to flee the palace forever.

"We tricked him!" they cried, and cackled with glee.

As for the crowds – they were enjoying the best procession ever. Boris, of course, wasn't having such a good day...

"Oh well," he thought, as he followed the emperor home. "At least one thing turned out as he wanted. People *will* talk about the emperor for years to come."

The Emperor's New Clothes was first told by Hans Christian Andersen, who was born in Denmark in 1805. He was the son of a poor shoemaker but grew up to write hundreds of fairy tales.

Series editor: Lesley Sims
Designed by Natacha Goransky
Cover design by Russell Punter

First published in 2005 by Usborne Publishing Ltd., Usborne House, 83-85 Saffron Hill, London EC1N 8RT, England. www.usborne.com
Copyright © 2005 Usborne Publishing Ltd.